Angelica
the Angel Fairy

Special thanks to Mandy Archer

ISBN 978-0-545-70828-9

10 9 8 7 6 5 4 3 2 1   15 16 17 18 19/0

Printed in the U.S.A.   40

First printing October 2015

Angelica
the Angel Fairy

by Daisy Meadows

SCHOLASTIC INC.

The Fairyland Palace

Seeing Pool

Tippington Town

Christmas angels shine and glitter,
But every year I grow more bitter.
Why does Santa only treat
Children who are kind and sweet?

Pretty gifts beneath the tree,
Those presents should belong to me!
Three magic objects in my fist
Will get my name on Santa's list.

Find the hidden letters in the stars throughout this book. Unscramble all 9 letters to spell a special word!

The Sparkly Panpipes

Contents

Winter Chaos

"The Winter Fair opens in five minutes," said Rachel Walker, her eyes dancing with excitement. "Are we ready to turn on the twinkle lights?"

"Definitely!" exclaimed her best friend, Kirsty Tate.

Kirsty was staying at Rachel's house for a few days of vacation. The pair had enjoyed a wonderful week ice-skating, drinking hot chocolates, and baking cookies. Time always seemed to fly by when Kirsty and Rachel were together!

Now it was Saturday afternoon and the friends were dressed in their Brownie uniforms. The girls in Rachel's troop had been working hard all morning — today was the day of the Tippington Brownies' Winter Fair! Kirsty and Rachel had volunteered to run the "winter woolies" stall, a tabletop stacked high with mittens, socks, and scarves knitted in rich, festive colors.

Rachel ran to the back of the hall. When one of the leaders gave the signal, she dimmed the main lights.

Everyone closed their eyes in the

darkness and counted
down together. "Three,
two, one . . . go!"

Flash!

There was a thrilled
gasp, then an explosion
of clapping and
cheering. The Brownies
had transformed Tippington's plain
old town hall into a magical winter
wonderland! Stalls lined every wall,
each one decorated with fake snow,
gold balls, and shiny bows. Strings
of glittery lights twinkled from the
ceiling. In the kitchen, Mrs. Walker and
the other Brownie moms had been busy
making hot chocolate and arranging
treats, filling the air with the smell of
warm cookies.

The girls had come in the day before to help deck the hall with lights, ribbons, and paper snowflakes.

Kirsty squeezed Rachel's hand and smiled. The friends shared a very special secret. From the very first day they met, the pair had been going on trips to Fairyland! They had shared some wonderful adventures with their magical friends. Both girls had made a promise to protect the fairies from Jack Frost and his grumpy goblins.

"Everybody to their positions, please," called their Brownie leader. "It's time to open the doors."

There was an excited hustle and bustle as the Brownies rushed to their stalls.

"We should raise lots of money today,"

said Kirsty hopefully. "Look at all these wonderful things!"

This year, the Brownies had decided to celebrate the true spirit of the holiday season. Instead of spending money on new equipment for the troop, they had chosen to buy gifts for people who weren't as lucky as they were. Giving to others was what this time of year was really all about.

"I can't wait to take a big sack of presents to Tippington Children's Hospital." Kirsty smiled. "It must be terrible to be sick at this time of year."

Rachel ran over to help another Brownie named Claire unpack the last few ornaments for her Christmas decoration stall.

"Don't forget the retirement-home visit, too!" she called back.

The Brownies had voted to spend half of the money on gifts for the children's hospital and the other half on the residents of the Greenacre Retirement Home, which was just around the corner from Rachel's house.

"Smile, everyone, please," called the Brownie leader, unbolting the hall doors.

Kirsty and Rachel swapped thrilled glances as the first shoppers trooped in

from the cold.
Soon there
were customers
wandering up
and down the
aisles, picking
up trinkets
and treating
themselves
to yummy
things to eat.

"You can be in charge of the money, Kirsty," suggested Rachel. "I'll put things in paper bags."

Both girls felt a little nervous at first, but soon they got the hang of things. Before long, the hall was full of people. If the afternoon continued like this, the fair would be a huge success!

When the line at their stall had calmed down a little, Kirsty walked across to Claire's decoration table.

"Claire, could I have some change," she whispered. "Claire? Oh!"

Kirsty's face flushed. Instead of selling decorations, Claire was swinging a piece of garland around. Passing shoppers had to duck out of her way, but their confused faces only made the Brownie burst into giggles.

"Look at me!" She laughed, knocking a tray of painted ornaments onto the floor.

Kirsty knelt down to pick them up. What was Claire doing?

Rachel rushed over to help. "Something's wrong," she whispered. "Come with me . . ."

An Old Fairy Friend

"Stand on this," said Rachel breathlessly, pulling a chair out from underneath the winter woolies table. "You'll get a better view."

Kirsty carefully climbed onto the chair and peered over the shoppers' heads.

"Everyone has abandoned their stalls!" She gasped. "And why is that girl munching cookies? They're supposed to be for sale!"

Instead of serving their customers, Brownies were running up and down the aisles, calling each other names and shrieking with laughter.

"Look at the twins," said Rachel, pointing to the stage.

Kirsty recognized Josie and Tilly from Rachel's last birthday party. They were supposed to be running the raffle. Ten people were waiting patiently to drop their tickets off, but the twins were ignoring them. The pair were far too busy helping themselves to the best prizes on the prize table.

"Every Brownie in the room is causing trouble," declared Kirsty. "At this rate we won't even raise a penny!"

As she stepped down from the chair, Rachel heard the tiniest tinkling sound.

"Is there something in your pocket?" she asked.

Kirsty shook her head. Then the tinkling sound chimed again! It was a little louder this time, like a delicate peal of silvery sleigh bells.

13

Rachel cupped her hand to her ear. There it was again! Kirsty began to gently lift up the gloves and scarves on the table, peeking hopefully underneath each one. She felt sure there must be a fairy nearby!

"Look at these," she whispered, holding up a set of pink knitted mittens.

Rachel's heart fluttered. "The sound is coming from inside!"

A stream of tiny musical notes shimmered around one of the mittens. The notes got brighter and brighter, until a little fairy popped her head out! Kirsty quickly turned the mitten around so no one else could see.

"Hello again!" said the fairy. "Happy holidays!"

Kirsty and Rachel beamed at each other. It was their old friend Melodie the Music Fairy. The last time they'd seen Melodie was at King  Oberon and Queen Titania's spectacular 1000th jubilee celebrations.

"Happy holidays to you, too!" Kirsty said.

"How lovely to see you," added Rachel, wondering if Melodie would know anything about the chaos at the Winter Fair. "Is everything all right in Fairyland?"

Melodie climbed out of the mitten and smoothed down her pretty pink dress.

"I'm afraid it's not." She frowned. "It's not all right at all!"

She explained that a very special musical instrument had been stolen from the Fairyland Palace.

"We've lost a set of sparkly panpipes. They belong to my friend Angelica the Angel Fairy, a wonderful fairy who uses her magic to help us all be as good as we can be. Without the sparkly panpipes, fairies and humans can't resist the temptation to cause trouble!" said Melodie.

"That explains why the Brownies are behaving so badly," said Rachel.

"I bet I know who took the pipes," whispered Kirsty. "Jack Frost!"

Melodie stretched out her gorgeous pink wings and fluttered up to the window ledge.

"You're right!" She nodded, perching on the ledge. "But that's not the only thing he's taken. Angelica also looks after a snow-white feather and an enchanted name scroll. Santa Claus himself uses the scroll to decide who deserves presents each year. Goodness knows what will happen on Christmas Eve if we don't get it back!"

"But that's only two days away!" cried Rachel. "We've got to do something!"

Kirsty agreed. "We can't waste a second."

Melodie's face lit up. "Oh, thank you!" She clapped her tiny hands. "Will you come with me to Fairyland? We can't let Jack Frost and his goblins get away with this!"

"Of course," chorused the girls.

Kirsty cupped the fairy in her hands, then followed Rachel to the big tree. No one would be able to see them behind it! When they were ready, Melodie waved her wand and the enchanting sleigh-bell tune instantly began to play once more. She gently touched each of the friends' heads with the tip of her wand, pink notes popping like glittering stars.

"Close your eyes," sang the fairy, her little voice perfectly in tune with the music.

The girls felt themselves being swept up and twirled high into the air. It was like riding a magical merry-go-round!

Seeing-Pool Secrets

Kirsty and Rachel opened their eyes to the most wonderful sight in the world. The best friends were hand in hand, sliding down a shimmering rainbow! The musical notes from Melodie's wand still sparkled and chimed all around them.

"We're fairies again!" whispered Kirsty excitedly.

Rachel wiggled her shoulders and smiled. A perfect pair of gossamer wings were gently uncurling on her back. As the rainbow arched down toward the clouds, she found herself flying along next to Melodie and Kirsty. The friends darted left and right, tumbling and twirling through the wintry sky.

Soon, red-and-white
toadstools came into
view below them,
dotted up and down
the snowy hillsides.
Rachel could even
see fairies fluttering
between the little homes!
She smiled and waved, but not one fairy
waved back.

"No one's very cheerful today,"
explained Melodie. "Some fairies
are even refusing to clean up their
toadstools!"

"Oh my," Rachel said. For a fairy, that
really was very bad behavior! Without
the sparkly panpipes, everyone was
struggling to be their normal, helpful
selves.

Melodie led the girls to the shining turrets of the Fairyland Palace.

"There's Angelica!" said Melodie, pointing to the Seeing Pool.

A lonely figure was perched on the edge of the pool, staring sadly into its frozen surface. Her softly feathered wings drooped. The girls could see her sweet face reflected on the ice, framed by a tumble of auburn curls.

"H-hello," said Angelica, doing her very best to smile. She was wearing a snow-white dress trimmed with swirling crystals. When the fairy stood up, her silk skirt swished gently around her.

"We came as soon as we heard," said
Rachel. "We're sorry that Jack Frost's
been up to no good again!"

Angelica's smile faded, her eyes
brimming with silvery tears.

"Each one of my magic objects is
truly precious." She
sighed.

The girls listened
carefully as Angelica
explained the objects'
special powers.

"The sparkly
panpipes bring peace,
and help everyone be well-behaved.
The snow-white feather is as pure as
our hearts, a symbol of harmony
that encourages us all to be gentle
and kind."

"And the enchanted scroll?" asked Kirsty, her eyes filled with concern.

Angelica put her face in her hands. "That is the most precious of all! The enchanted scroll records the names of every fairy and child who has been good. I give the scroll to Santa every Christmas Eve before he loads up his sleigh."

Melodie put her arm around Angelica's shoulders.

"If Santa doesn't have his list of good children," Angelica added, "he won't know where to deliver his presents!"

Rachel remembered all the children staying in Tippington Hospital. Unless she and Kirsty could help Angelica, their Christmas wouldn't be happy or peaceful this year!

"Don't worry," she said. "We'll make sure Jack Frost gives everything back."

Kirsty nodded, adding, "And before Christmas, too!"

Angelica's face filled with hope. "Melodie promised you would help. Thank you so much!"

At that very moment, a ray of sunlight passed over the Seeing Pool. A stunning golden firebird soared above the fairies' heads, its plumes the color of flames.

"Hey!" called a voice. "Wait for me!"

A fairy in a flowing orange dress glided down to join the group. It was Erin the Phoenix Fairy, rushing to keep up with her best friend, Giggles! As soon as she saw Kirsty and Rachel, Erin's face lit up.

"We've come to find Jack Frost," said Kirsty, "but we're not sure where to start."

"Why don't we ask the Seeing Pool?" suggested Erin, beckoning to Giggles.

The firebird touched the edge of the

pool with the tip of his tail feather and the ice instantly melted. The waters swirled, then parted to reveal a picture.

"Look!" cried Angelica.

Rachel peered into the pool and shivered. There was Jack Frost in his castle, blowing noisily on Angelica's sparkly panpipes! His goblins hooted and laughed as he paraded up and down, blowing with all his might.

"Those panpipes are fragile!" pointed out Melodie. "What if Jack Frost breaks them?"

"We won't let him," insisted Kirsty.

"We've got to go to the Ice Castle right away," agreed Rachel. "Right this very second!"

Toot, Toot, Toot!

There was just enough time for Kirsty and Rachel to give Melodie and Erin a quick farewell hug before Angelica whisked them away to Jack Frost's Ice Castle.

The friends fluttered nervously above the castle's jagged towers, which stood cold and unwelcoming in the bitter breeze. Down below them, dozens of goblins stomped noisily around the ramparts.

"This way!" cried Kirsty, pointing to a crooked turret on the far wing. It was dripping in icicles, each one razor-sharp. The fairies darted into the tower through a cracked window.

"Toot-toot-tooooot!"

Inside, the tower echoed with the din of Jack Frost's terrible pipe-playing. The fairies summoned up all their courage, then fluttered toward the terrible sound.

The flights of steps spiraled down and
down, finally coming to a stop in front
of a pair of huge iron doors. Two goblin
guards stood in front, clamping their
mittens over their big green ears.

"What a racket!" complained one.
"He's been hooting
and tooting all
morning!"

"When
will it stop?"
yelled
the other,
scrunching
up his eyes.

The
fairies pressed
themselves against
the cold stone wall.

"That's the Throne Room," whispered Rachel. "The next time the doors open, try and slip in behind the guards."

Angelica and Kirsty both nodded in agreement.

Suddenly a muffled voice started shouting from inside the Throne Room.

"Where are my new decorations?" barked Jack Frost. "Take this trash away!"

"Some people are never happy!" grumbled a goblin.

Suddenly the great doors creaked opened, giving the fairies the chance they needed. As the goblin scuttled out, Kirsty, Rachel, and Angelica darted noiselessly into the hall. Jack Frost was standing in the center of the chamber, shouting and stamping his foot. A gaggle of goblins scowled and sulked in the corner.

"I can see my sparkly panpipes," said Angelica in a hushed voice. "They're in his hand!"

The fairies quickly hid themselves in the dazzling ice chandelier that hung over the throne. Kirsty perched herself on a diamond droplet just above Jack Frost's head.

"What happened in here?" she wondered, looking around.

The Throne Room had been decorated for the holidays, but not in a way that the girls had ever seen before. Instead of brightening up the walls with tinsel and holly wreaths, the goblins had strung up spiderwebs and thorns! In one corner a spiky dead tree had been clumsily propped up in an old bucket.

"Those pesky fairies say this instrument will make anyone well-behaved," snorted Jack Frost, tooting on the panpipes as hard as he could. "What a pack of lies! You goblins are even more useless than usual!"

"So what?" a goblin retorted, shrugging his shoulders.

Jack Frost's face turned white with rage.

"So what?" he bellowed. "I told you I wanted the finest decorations in the kingdom and what do I get? Moldy webs and a tree that's just a dead twig!"

The dim-witted goblins looked over at the sorry tree, then burst into fits of laughter.

"I bet there won't be many presents under *that* this year!" said one.

Jack Frost kicked the tree so hard that it fell to the ground.

"Angelica!" he yelled furiously. "Those panpipes don't work!"

Angelica couldn't stand to hear another word. The brave little fairy burst out of the chandelier, making the crystals ripple and chime.

"My panpipes are supposed to make people well-behaved," she said angrily. "They don't make people obey selfish commands!"

Pipes of Peace

"Angelica!" Kirsty cried in dismay. "Be careful!"

Rachel reached for her friend's hand. "We have to help her."

Angelica fluttered left and right, still trying to reason with a furious Jack Frost.

"I would never tell a lie," she said earnestly. "The sparkly panpipes will only work if you play them the right way."

"Tooot-toot-tooot!"

Rachel watched in astonishment.
Jack Frost
wasn't
listening to
a word that
Angelica was
saying!

"He still hasn't
seen her." She gasped.
"He's too busy
shouting and making
that terrible noise!"

The friends darted behind the frozen
throne. In between blasting out-of-
tune toots on the panpipes, Jack Frost
continued to bark and bellow at his
goblins. The goblins argued back just as
loudly. Not one of them stopped to

notice the tiny fairy pleading to be
heard. At last, poor Angelica had to
give up.

"He thought the panpipes would
make the goblins obey his every
command," she told her friends, "but
they're being even more troublesome
than usual!"

Kirsty looked
thoughtful for a
moment, before
starting to smile.
She'd just had a
fantastic idea!

"I know how
to get Jack Frost's
attention," she said,
"but it's not going to
be easy."

Rachel and Angelica listened intently as their friend proposed that they should each use their hands to block the ends of the sparkly panpipes. Kirsty had counted that the magic instrument had six pipes tied together with silver thread — one for each fairy hand! The difficult part would be flying close enough to Jack Frost without getting batted away or even worse, caught!

"If he hears that his plan won't work, he might be persuaded to give the panpipes back," said Rachel hopefully.

Angelica nodded. "It's worth a try."

The threesome fluttered out into the middle of the Throne Room.

"You goblins had better fix that tree or I'll . . . I'll . . . What's that?" Jack Frost scowled. "Fairies in my Ice Castle?"

Kirsty and Rachel darted to one side, just missing a flick from Jack Frost's bony finger. Angelica whirled around the other way, grasping the end of the sparkly panpipes with both hands.

Jack Frost lifted the enchanted instrument to his lips, with Angelica still clinging on.

"I'll show you!" he roared, blowing as hard as he could.

"Come on, Rachel!" shouted Kirsty, flying up to put her hands over two more holes.

Jack Frost swung the panpipes from side to side, but Kirsty and Angelica held on tight.

"Almost there!" puffed Rachel, flitting from left to right.

At last she managed to flutter in and clutch on to the last two pipes. The furious hooting and tooting stopped at once. Jack gasped in surprise.

"Well done, girls!" said Angelica with a proud smile. She flew up to face Jack Frost. "Now, if you'd just listen, I can tell you exactly why the panpipes aren't working."

Jack Frost
waited sulkily
as Angelica
had her say.
When he
realized
that she was
telling the truth
his mouth twisted
into a scowl.

"Will you give the sparkly panpipes
back now?" demanded Rachel. "They're
no use to you."

Jack Frost replied with a rude noise
and tossed the precious object to the
floor. Angelica dashed down to catch it.

"Watch out!" pleaded Kirsty. A clumsy
goblin was lifting up his enormous foot
at just the wrong moment!

Angelica touched the panpipes with the tip of her wand in the nick of time. A cascade of golden stars whirled around the magic object, shrinking it down to fairy-size. Angelica tucked the pipes under her arm, then fluttered back to join her friends.

"Let's get you back to Tippington," she said breathlessly. "They'll be needing you at the Winter Fair!"

Despite its sorry start, the Brownie sale was going strong now. Happy shoppers strolled up and down the aisles, chatting with friends and neighbors. The Brownie leader stood proudly in front of the tree, watching her girls happily serve all the shoppers.

"It's just wonderful," Angelica cooed.

"Can you stay for a while?" asked Rachel, finding a cozy hiding spot for the fairy on the winter woolies stall.

"I'd love to," replied Angelica. "Without

you, Jack Frost would still have the enchanted panpipes!"

The little fairy lifted the magic instrument to her lips. As she started to play a beautiful song, people began to gather around Kirsty and Rachel's stall.

"Look out the window," whispered Rachel to her friend.

Kirsty looked, and her face shone with happiness. Outside the hall, the first snowflakes of winter were gently starting to fall.

"I have a feeling that this is going to be our most successful Brownie Fair ever!" Kirsty beamed.

Rachel grinned back at her best friend. "I couldn't agree more!"

The Snow- White Feather

Contents

Sunshine and Snowflakes

"I love snow!" declared Kirsty, cupping a handful in her gloves and shaping it into a snowball.

"Tippington has turned into a snowy wonderland!" Rachel said.

She giggled as Kirsty sent the snowball tumbling through the air. It disappeared into a holly bush dotted with scarlet berries, making the leaves rustle and sparkle in the light.

It really was a beautiful day to be outside. A steady layer of snowflakes had been falling silently ever since the Brownie sale. The town's white paths and rooftops twinkled brightly like a picture on a pretty holiday card.

Kirsty slipped an arm through Rachel's. "It all started with Angelica's visit," she whispered, thinking of the new fairy friend they had met the day before.

Rachel nodded enthusiastically. The golden sunbeams dancing on the snow reminded her of Angelica the Angel Fairy's tumbling auburn curls.

The girls trudged on through the snowy streets, taking in the magic. Kirsty, Rachel, and all the other Brownies were on their way to deliver holiday gifts to the residents of the Greenacre

Retirement Home. Under their snuggly coats everyone was dressed nicely in their uniforms.

"We're here, Kirsty!" said Rachel, pointing to a large Victorian house at the end of a sweeping drive.

The Brownie leader led the troop up the drive. A beautiful wreath twinkled above the front door.

"I can't wait to see the residents' faces when they spot our baskets of goodies." Kirsty beamed, her cheeks rosy with cold.

The friends had enjoyed a wonderful morning wrapping up presents for the retirees living in the home. Both girls had puts lots of thought into every gift. Lace handkerchiefs, gloves, diaries, and bottles of bubble bath had all been carefully wrapped, and decorated with ribbon and gift tags.

The Brownies waited patiently, stamping their feet in the snow. At last the door swung open and a woman with a friendly face stepped out to greet them.

"Welcome!" she cried.

The woman introduced herself as Mrs. Pepper, the owner of the retirement home. She led the girls into the lobby and showed them where to hang their coats.

"Can you hear that?" whispered Kirsty, as soon as they got inside.

Rachel listened for a minute. The muffled sound of singing echoed down the hallway.

"The residents are listening to music in the common room," explained Mrs. Pepper. "The old records are their favorites!"

Mrs. Pepper showed the Brownies into a cozy room, which had a fire roaring in the grate. A group of ladies and gentlemen sat in a semicircle around a record player, listening to a bright, festive tune.

"Hello!" said Rachel, eager to meet everyone.

A gray-haired man scowled at her, then hid behind his newspaper.

Kirsty knelt down beside an old lady in a blue dress.

"My favorite carol is 'Silent Night,'" she said. "What's yours?"

The old lady glared at Kirsty, then harrumphed very loudly and turned to face the window.

Kirsty and Rachel glanced at each other in surprise. This wasn't the welcome they had been expecting!

"Come on," suggested Kirsty in a low voice, "let's put the presents under the tree."

The girls quietly started to unpack the gifts from their baskets and stack them under the tree in the corner.

"Hey, you!" called a voice.

"Yes?" asked Rachel, leaping up with a smile.

A tiny old lady wearing a pair of glasses on a chain scowled back at her.

"Can you move?" she snapped. "I can't see the tree with your head in the way!"

Before poor Rachel could think of an answer, another woman pulled herself up to her feet.

"Edith Smythe!" she bellowed. "You're wearing my glasses!"

"Well, they're mine now!" insisted Mrs. Smythe.

The lady made a swipe for the glasses chain, but Mrs. Smythe batted her hand out of the way. The Brownies watched in stunned silence as the pair began to make faces and call each other names.

Other residents started to join in the ruckus, too. A gentleman in a green cardigan snatched his neighbor's hearing aid, then three old ladies began to squabble about who had the best chair. The shouting got so loud it was even drowning out the record player's music. Instead of behaving like grandparents, the old people were acting like grumpy toddlers!

An Unexpected Visitor

"There's not much holiday spirit in here."
Kirsty frowned. "I think Jack Frost has
been causing trouble again."

Rachel nodded in agreement. She had
been thinking the exact same thing!

"This has got to stop," she said, rushing
over to the record player and lifting up
the needle. If she could just get the
residents' attention, she might be able to
persuade them to calm down and be nice
to one another!

The vinyl record stopped spinning, but somehow the song continued to play.

Rachel gasped in astonishment. "It must be fairy magic!"

Kirsty's heart skipped a beat. The festive tune still echoed through the speakers. Every time the chorus hit a high note, a tiny golden star appeared in the air. Each star glittered for a moment, before shimmering out of sight.

"Those stars are getting brighter," remarked Rachel, standing in front of the speakers to hide the twinkling lights. The room was in such chaos that nobody even noticed.

The stars began to fizz even more brightly. Suddenly a flash of gold zoomed past the friends so fast it made them blink.

"Oh!" gasped a tinkly voice. "It's even worse than I thought!"

Kirsty and Rachel opened their eyes immediately. There was Angelica the Angel Fairy, fluttering in the air in front of them! In an instant the little fairy was gone again, darting across to the tree. She tucked herself in among the thick pine branches at the back, then motioned for the girls to come over.

Kirsty and Rachel put the record back on, then rushed over to the tree.

"It's the snow-white feather, isn't it?" whispered Kirsty, crouching down. "Everyone here is being so mean!"

"Yes." Angelica nodded. "I came as soon as I heard."

The fairy's little heart-shaped face looked pale with worry.  She explained how she'd just met Gabriella the Snow Kingdom Fairy flying over the hills of Fairyland.

"Gabriella warned me that she'd spotted a group of goblins heading to the human world." She sighed. "So I decided to follow them. I knew they would be up to no good! Ever since we rescued the sparkly panpipes from Jack Frost's Ice Castle he's been trying to find somewhere to hide the other magic objects."

"The goblins led you here?" asked Rachel.

"That's right," said Angelica breathlessly. "They've got to be somewhere inside Greenacre."

"*Achoo!*"

Kirsty and Rachel sprang to their feet. A rather strange-looking worker in a green uniform wobbled into the common room, pushing a clanking snack cart.

"*ACHOO!*"

The worker sneezed again, barging his way through the Brownies and residents. The very loud sneeze matched the stranger's very large nose. An old lady put down her knitting and demanded a cup of tea, but the worker completely ignored her.

"Look what he's doing!" Rachel gasped, her eyes wide with shock.

Instead of serving drinks, the worker leaned across the cart and yanked the top off the cookie tin. He began to shove handfuls of cookies into his mouth, gobbling down three at a time.

"Isn't he supposed to

be passing those out to the residents?"
said Kirsty.

Angelica fluttered out from behind a
twinkle light.

"We've found our first goblin," she
announced, her eyes dancing with
excitement.

Rachel and Kirsty edged a little
closer to the goblin. Milk and tea were
splattered all over the cart, but they
couldn't see the snow-white feather
anywhere. When the greedy goblin had
shoved every last cookie into his mouth,
he began to push his way back out of the
door. There was only one thing to do.

"Follow that goblin!" the girls cried
together.

A Thousand Feathers!

Kirsty pointed to the golden piece
of tinsel tied around Rachel's blonde
ponytail.

"Angelica," she said urgently, "do
you think you can hide yourself at the
back of Rachel's hair? The bow should
cover you."

Angelica gave her wand a bold little wave to show that she was ready. The girls carefully helped the tiny fairy wiggle in between the loops of tinsel wrapped around Rachel's ponytail. She tucked herself in so beautifully, even Kirsty had a hard time spotting her.

"Let's go!" called Angelica in a tinkly voice no louder than a whisper.

The friends picked their way across the room, stepping in between the angry residents and flustered Brownies.

"Hurry!" urged Rachel, slipping out of the door just before their leader and Mrs. Pepper wandered inside.

Farther down the hallway, the wheels on the snack cart rattled and squeaked. Kirsty and Rachel ran after it, ducking into doorways whenever the goblin stopped to sneeze or scratch his nose. Suddenly a loud *bang!* echoed down the corridor.

Angelica pushed her head out of the tinsel and stretched her wings.

"He went into that storage room and slammed the door!" she cried, anxiously doing a loop-the-loop.

Butterflies flipped in Kirsty's stomach. She took a deep breath, then grabbed the doorknob firmly and twisted it open.

"Oh!" Kirsty cried.

The storage room door swung open to reveal not one, not two, but *three* goblins! They were playing around with the retirement home's medical equipment, hooting with laughter. The first goblin

had pulled off his uniform and was now picking up bandages and throwing them at his friends' heads. Another one was making a lot of noise as he raced around and around in a wheelchair. He skidded into chairs and cabinets, cackling at every crash.

"The snow-white feather can't be in here," Angelica whispered in dismay. "Those goblins are being far too thoughtless!"

"What's happening in the corner?" wondered Kirsty, staring at a goblin with pointy ears.

The mischievous goblin barged through a row of walkers, knocking them in all directions. Then he stacked them back up, one on top of another, and climbed up. The tower wobbled and swayed under the goblin's weight.

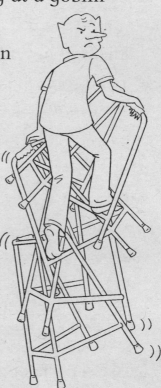

"I bet I can reach the ceiling!" he yelled, blowing a raspberry.

"Those walkers are going to be ruined if he keeps doing that!" said Rachel, putting her hands on her hips. She stepped into the storage room, then coughed loudly. *"Ahem!"*

The goblin with the pointy ears jumped so high he banged his head on the ceiling! The whole stack of walkers clattered down to the floor, causing a terrible racket.

"Owwww!" he groaned, heaving the walkers off his body.

His two friends yanked him up by the arms. They'd already spotted Angelica fluttering in the doorway!

"Get up!" yelled the first goblin. "We've got to get out of here!"

The second goblin elbowed his way through the door.

"Trust a pesky fairy to ruin our fun," he muttered, swiping at Angelica as he barged down the corridor. The little fairy darted out of reach, leaving a trail of golden swirls shimmering in the air behind her.

"Are you all right?" asked Rachel,
when the goblins had passed.

"Yes, thank you!"
said Angelica.
"Thanks for
interrupting those
troublemakers.
That was really
brave!"

Kirsty gave
her best friend's
hand a proud
squeeze.

"This way!"
Angelica cried.
"They're heading toward the bedrooms."
The girls hurried along the corridor
just a few yards behind the stomping
goblins. The silly threesome pushed and

shoved one another to get to the front, knocking into picture frames and bashing against doors. The goblins argued loudly all the way, not caring about the commotion they were making.

Soon the goblin with the pointy ears couldn't help boasting again. "I'm the best climber *and* I'm the best hider, too!" he teased, making a face at the others.

The first goblin scratched his head. "What do you mean?"

"I found the perfect place for that magic feather," he bragged. "Take a look in here!"

The goblin threw open a bedroom door and ushered his friends inside. Angelica, Rachel, and Kirsty slipped in behind them, their hearts racing with excitement.

"Oh no!" cried Kirsty.

The bedroom was filled with even more goblins, who were having an enormous pillow

fight! Jack Frost's goblins were hitting one another so hard that the pillows were bursting. Feathers tumbled and swirled in every direction.

Silvery tears sprang to Angelica's eyes. "There must be a thousand snow-white feathers in here," she exclaimed. "Which one is mine?"

Mischief and Mayhem

The room looked terrible. Soft white
feathers floated around the room like a
swirling snowstorm. A pair of goblins
jumped up and down on the bed. They
swung pillows at the goblins on the floor.
Another hung from the light fixture,
knocking other goblins over with his
enormous green feet.

Angelica fluttered to
the nightstand, then
signaled for Kirsty
and Rachel to tiptoe
along the wall and
duck down beside her.
"What do we do now?"
Angelica asked. Finding one
special feather among all this
mayhem would be impossible!

The goblin with the pointy ears didn't
seem too happy about all the extra
feathers, either.

"Oh no!" he shouted. "You've messed
up my hiding place."

One of the other goblins chuckled.
"What's Jack Frost going to say?" he
taunted. "Bet he won't be so proud of
you now!"

The pointy-eared goblin poked him in the chest.

"That's not true!" he yelled. "I stashed it in the bottom pillow in the corner. How was I supposed to know that all of you would come in and mix everything up? You'd better help me look for it or we'll all be in trouble."

The anxious goblin began to pick up pillows one by one, turning them upside down and shaking the cases until feathers settled all over the carpet. His friends reluctantly joined in.

"Not in this one," the pointy-eared goblin muttered, "or in this one, or this one."

Rachel shook her head at the foolish goblins.

"Now there are even *more* feathers flying around the room," she said.

"We'd better start looking, too," said Kirsty, picking up a pillowcase and peeking inside. "What else can we do?"

Angelica's little voice began to tremble. "What about all these goblins?" she asked nervously.

"If we stay in the corner we should be all right," said Rachel gently. "Most of them are too busy fighting to notice us."

The friends started searching. Kirsty and Rachel sifted through handfuls of feathers, hoping to spot one that stood out from the rest. Angelica danced around like a golden sunbeam, her beautiful curls bobbing as she flew. They looked and looked until their eyes got tired, but the enchanted snow-white feather was nowhere to be seen.

On the other side of the bedroom, the goblin with the pointy ears had already given up.

"This is a waste of time," he grumbled. "I can't believe you all lost the feather!"

"Don't blame me!" bellowed the goblin next to him, hitting him on the nose with a half-stuffed pillow.

The pointy- eared goblin grabbed the pillow and hit his rival on the bottom. It was such a perfect shot that the goblins on the bed stopped to applaud.

"Fight! Fight!" they whooped, their eyes gleaming.

The pair didn't need telling twice. They were soon thumping each other with such force that a new flurry of feathers tumbled to the floor.

Angelica squealed with delight. "There it is!"

One snow-white plume shimmered as it fell silently to the ground. A haze of silver fairy dust twinkled all around it, glittering like crystals.

Kirsty and Rachel scrambled to catch the feather, but the pointy-eared goblin got there first.

"I'll take that!" he roared, seizing the precious object in his big green hands.

A Helpful Goblin

"Be careful!" wailed Rachel, as the goblin's fingers closed around Angelica's treasured possession. "The snow-white feather is very delicate!"

Kirsty stepped forward to support her friend, adding, "And it doesn't belong to you!"

"You again?" grunted the goblin. "You'll never get this feather!"

The smug goblin lifted his arms up above the girls' heads so they couldn't reach the feather. Angelica flitted after it, then perched precariously on his thumb.

"Please let it go," she begged, desperately trying to unpeel the goblin's fingers.

The pointy-eared goblin tried to sneer at the fairy, but his expression didn't come out quite right. The other pillow fighters nudged one another. The goblin's face was beginning to relax into a calm smile.

"That's the magic of the snow-white feather," Angelica explained gently. "It makes everyone kind and gentle — *even* grumpy goblins!"

Kirsty and Rachel's eyes lit up. No wonder this magic object was so precious!

The little fairy tapped the goblin's hand with her wand.

"Excuse me," she said quietly. "May I have my feather back, please?"

The goblin nodded his head and politely bowed to Angelica. Rachel had to stifle a giggle.

"I've never seen such good goblin behavior," she whispered to Kirsty.

Her best friend beamed. Jack Frost would not be impressed at all! The goblin graciously opened his palm. Angelica gave the snow-white feather the slightest touch with the tip of her golden wand. In an instant it had shrunk back down to fairy-size.

"That's better," she cooed, holding the tiny plume between her finger and thumb.

The delighted fairy twirled back to her friends, her cheeks flushed with pleasure.

"That was a surprise." Kirsty grinned.
The pointy-eared goblin's eyes were as
wide as saucers. He was still standing
with his hand outstretched, wondering
 where his feather
had gone! As
soon as the
magic
object
was out
of his
grasp, his
troublesome
goblin streak
returned.
"Did I just do what I think I did?" he
wailed.
The other goblins grabbed him by the
arm and hurried him toward the door.

"Yes, you did!" grumbled the first goblin, shaking his head in disappointment.

"What did you go and do that for?" snapped the other one. "Jack Frost will be hopping mad when he hears you've been helping the fairies."

The pointy-eared goblin's face crumpled.

"Helping fairies?" he howled. "I've never been so ashamed!"

The rest of the goblins dropped their pillows and made a run for it. They wanted to get back to the Ice Castle before Jack Frost heard the bad news!

They shoved their way past the girls, slamming the door behind them.

"Phew!" Rachel breathed a sigh of relief when the coast was clear. "That's one way to scare off a goblin!"

Angelica burst into a peal of fairy giggles. "Thank you so much, girls." She beamed. "His face did look pretty funny."

Before
Angelica
took the
snow-white
feather
back to
Fairyland,
she had one
last job to do.
She waved her
wand with a
little flourish.

"How pretty!"
Kirsty sighed as a stream of twinkly
fairy dust swirled around the room.
When the sparkles had settled, all the
pillows were plumped up and back on
the beds again. There wasn't a stray
feather in sight!

Kirsty and
Rachel
waved
good–bye to
Angelica,
then made
their way
back to
Greenacre's
common room.

"It's even
better than we
could have hoped," gushed Rachel,
peeking inside.

Now that the snow-white feather was
out of goblin hands, the home's residents
had stopped arguing. Instead they were
gathered around the tree, listening to the
Brownies singing their favorite carols.

Mrs. Pepper and their Brownie leader stood by the fire, their faces bright and smiling.

Kirsty and Rachel took their places in the group and joined in with the singing.

Everyone was having a magical time! The fun had only just begun, too. As the last chorus trailed off, the excited Brownies made their way toward the tree.

"Come on, Kirsty," exclaimed Rachel. "Let's hand out those presents!"

The Enchanted Name Scroll

Contents

Christmas Countdown

"So what have you put on your
Christmas list, Billy?" asked Kirsty,
perching on the end of a hospital bed.

A little boy in dinosaur pajamas
clapped his hands with excitement.

"A Tyrannosaurus rex!" he announced.
"A really big one!"

Rachel's eyes twinkled. "Have you
been good this year?"

Billy nodded proudly. It was Christmas Eve and Rachel's Brownie troop had come to visit the patients at Tippington Children's Hospital. The corridors looked cozy and bright, covered from floor to ceiling in paper decorations and twinkling lights. Doctors wandered up and down in Santa hats, checking charts and handing out medicine. Garlands of tinsel sparkled around the nurses' stations and festive tunes echoed down the wards.

"I can't wait to see the children's faces when they see what we've brought!" Rachel said.

Rachel pulled out a little pencil and notebook from her uniform pocket, then wrote down Billy's name. The Brownie

troop had used the money raised at the Winter Fair to buy toys for the boys and girls who were too sick to go home for the holidays.

Now the Brownies needed to make sure that each patient got something that they would enjoy. The hospital playroom was stacked with trains, cars, teddy bears, and tea sets. Each toy had been carefully wrapped in bright paper and tied with curly ribbon.

"Do you remember the plastic dinosaur with the green tail?" asked Kirsty. "That would be a perfect present for Billy!"

Rachel crossed the toy dino off her list, then slipped the notebook back in her pocket.

Kirsty wandered over to say hello to a small girl whose leg was in a plaster cast. "I'm Kirsty, what's your name?"

"I'm Emily," replied the girl in a shy voice. "I broke my leg ice-skating."

Kirsty gave Emily's hand a friendly squeeze. "You poor thing," she said. "Maybe Santa

will bring you something extra-special this year!"

The little patient's eyes suddenly glistened with tears. "How is he going to know where to deliver the presents?" she asked. "I didn't think I'd be here on Christmas morning."

"Santa never gets things wrong," replied Rachel. "He's got a special list."

"I hope so." Emily sighed, sinking back on her pillow. "I don't know what I'd do if Santa forgot about me."

Rachel tried to look cheerful, but inside, her heart gave a little flutter. She wondered what would happen if they didn't find Angelica's enchanted name scroll before bedtime.

Kirsty looked worried, too. There were only hours to go before Santa Claus would be leaving his workshop at the North Pole. Although Angelica had two of her magic objects back, Jack Frost was still hiding the fairy's precious scroll. The scroll contained the names of all the children who had been good. If Angelica didn't give the scroll to Santa, he wouldn't know where to deliver his presents.

"What did you wish for?" asked Kirsty, taking a quick peek out the hospital window. The sky was already dark. Snowflakes fell silently over the town.

Emily's eyes shone hopefully. "I'd love a fairy doll," she gushed.

Just then, a nurse in navy slacks wheeled a food cart into the ward. On her shirt a Christmas-tree brooch flashed

merrily next to a
name badge that
read SALLY.

"Dinnertime!"
called Nurse Sally.
"Who would like a
sandwich and a slice
of chocolate Yule log?"
While the Brownie
leader and the rest of the troop helped
pass around the trays of food, Kirsty led
Rachel a little way up the corridor.

"We can't let Emily and the others
down," she whispered. "We have to find
the enchanted name scroll. It's almost
time for Santa to load up his sleigh."

Rachel nodded. "I'd hoped it would
have turned up by now. I don't even
know where to start looking."

Just then, three hospital aides in white coats tumbled out of a side room. They marched toward Rachel and Kirsty, their eyes fixed on the floor. *Bash!* The clumsy trio knocked right into Nurse Sally's food cart. The nurse gasped as the cart careened down the corridor.

"Careful!" Rachel frowned, running over to help.

The friends caught the food cart just in time, but the workers didn't even bother to apologize.

"What are you three doing here anyway?" demanded Nurse Sally, putting her hands on her hips. "I didn't call for any helpers!"

The strange workers muttered something under their breath. Then the tallest one broke into an awkward run, pushing past Rachel as he bolted for the door.

Rachel shivered. "That was Jack Frost," she gasped. "He's here!"

A Flicker of Fairy Magic

"Are you sure it was Jack Frost?" whispered Kirsty.

"I'm positive," insisted Rachel. "He was freezing cold. I bet he's brought a couple of goblins with him, too!"

Kirsty wheeled the cart back into the middle of the ward. As soon as Nurse Sally and the Brownies were busy again giving out the children's dinners, the girls snuck out of the room. If Jack Frost was lurking in the Tippington Children's Hospital, they needed to find him fast! The girls tiptoed past the nurses' station and then pushed through the ward's double doors.

"There he is!" exclaimed Kirsty.

Now that they were out of the grown-ups' sight, Jack Frost and his goblins didn't even bother to try and disguise themselves. Their big clumpy feet clattered down the corridor, making a terrible noise. The threesome bumped and jostled all the way, eyeing each other with grumpy faces.

"Come on!" yelled Jack Frost, tugging the nearest goblin by the shirt. "Santa won't wait much longer!"

Jack Frost dug a hand into his coat pocket and pulled out a golden roll of parchment tied with a red velvet ribbon.

Kirsty and Rachel both gasped in surprise. It had to be Angelica's enchanted name scroll! Before the girls could get any closer, a doctor strolled down the corridor. Quick as a flash, Jack Frost ducked into an empty side room.

"Where'd he go?" wondered one of the goblins, wrinkling his long nose.

The other goblin scratched his head. "Don't ask me!"

The doctor stared at the strange pair. Just when it seemed like he was going to say something, an icy hand reached out of the side room and dragged the goblins inside. The door slammed shut behind them. The doctor shrugged, then smiled at Kirsty and Rachel. As soon as he had

passed, the girls rushed up to the closed
door and peered through the window set
into it. Inside they could see Jack Frost
and his goblins huddled in a corner. All
three were talking
in urgent voices,
pointing and
glaring at the
enchanted
scroll.

"They're
definitely up
to no good."
Rachel frowned.
"We can't let them
do anything to ruin Santa's list!"

As she spoke, the string of twinkle
lights on the wall above her seemed to
flare even brighter.

"We're going to have to go in there,"
said Kirsty, pushing against the door.

Rachel caught her friend's arm. There
was no doubt about it — the lights were
blinking faster now, too!

"I wonder," she said in a hushed voice.
"Could Angelica be close by?"

The girls held hands —
both hoping to see some
fairy magic. A glittering
swoosh of gold burst out
from the lights, sending
sparkles spiraling in
all directions.
Angelica the Angel
Fairy fluttered into
view, a tiny trail of
fairy dust cascading
behind her. Her

cheeks had flushed the color of pink
rosebuds.

"Kirsty! Rachel!" she exclaimed. "I
didn't think I'd get here in time!"

The friends said a quick hello, thrilled
to be together again.

"The scroll is in there . . ." whispered
Rachel urgently,
keeping her voice
as low as she
could.

". . . in Jack
Frost's hands!"
finished Kirsty.

Angelica
gasped. "As soon
as I heard that Jack
Frost was on his way
to the human world, I decided

to follow him," she announced in a brave voice. "What is he doing in a children's hospital?"

A noisy shout rang out from the side room.

"This piece of paper is useless," bellowed Jack Frost, "just like you goblins!"

"Watch out!" Kirsty gasped, pulling Rachel back from the door.

The door swung back on its hinges with a deafening thud. Angelica darted up into the twinkle lights just as Jack Frost came thundering into view. Kirsty and Rachel pressed themselves against the wall.

The two goblins ran into the corridor, too. They craned their heads left and

right, but the pair didn't think to look behind them!

"Get me a pen, NOW!" shouted Jack Frost. "My name needs to be scrawled on that list in the biggest letters Santa's ever seen!"

The Name Game

As soon as Jack Frost and his goblins had crashed back down the corridor, Rachel stood up on her tiptoes.

"Angelica," she called gently. "It's safe to come out now."

The little fairy flitted out of her hiding spot.

"We need to get closer to Jack Frost," she decided. "It sounds like he's about to do something very selfish."

Rachel felt a little frightened at the thought of eavesdropping on Jack Frost — what would happen if they got caught?

"It's not going to be easy," Kirsty said. "These long corridors don't have many hiding places when you're our size."

Angelica pointed to her wand. "How would you like to be fairies again?" she asked.

Both girls shared a delighted smile.

"Oh, yes, please," replied Rachel. "That would make things much easier!"

Angelica twirled her wand in a circle, sending a cloud of fairy dust dancing in all directions. The friends watched as the sprinkles began to settle in their hair. Rachel took a deep breath. The fairy dust smelled of everything she loved about the holidays — pine trees, gingerbread, and candy canes all rolled into one!

"I can feel myself shrinking!" declared Kirsty as a glistening pair of wings magically appeared on her back. The delicate pink wings were so pale she could almost see through them.

Rachel shrugged her shoulders and felt her own wings begin to open and close gently. "Isn't it wonderful?" she said.

The friends could have tumbled and twirled through the air all day, but they didn't dare waste another second. They flew straight up to Angelica's side and listened carefully to her instructions.

"Follow me down the corridor," she said. "Try and fly as high as you can. If we stay close to the decorations, Jack Frost shouldn't notice us."

"Good idea," agreed Kirsty.

One by one, the fairies flitted down the corridor, darting in and out of the paper chains and tinsel.

It didn't take long to track down Jack Frost and his goblins. They had wandered into a ward that had been closed for the Christmas break. The three stood at the end of an empty hospital bed, hunched over the mattress.

"Oh, my!" Angelica gasped.

Rachel and Kirsty fluttered down and perched on the head of the bedframe, just out of sight. The goblins had stretched the enchanted scroll out so that Jack Frost could write his name at the top! He tried again and again to make a mark on the magic parchment, but nothing seemed to work.

"I need another pen!" he growled. "Now!"

The goblin with the long nose rolled his eyes.

"We've given you dozens already," he grumbled. "Felt-tips, ballpoints, markers — you've tried them all!"

The other goblin groaned. "You've been scribbling on that scroll ever since you took it from Fairyland. Can't we just go back to the Ice Castle?"

Jack Frost threw the pen on the floor. "Silence!" he ordered. "I need to get my name on that list. Why else do you think we're in a hospital?"

"Oh my!" Angelica gasped.

Rachel and Kirsty fluttered down and perched on the head of the bedframe, just out of sight. The goblins had stretched the enchanted scroll out so that Jack Frost could write his name at the top! He tried again and again to make a mark on the magic parchment, but nothing seemed to work.

"I need another pen!" he growled. "Now!"

The goblin with the long nose rolled his eyes.

Jack Frost want his name on Santa's list of good children anyway?" she asked.

"Easy!" declared Rachel. "He's after an extra-big pile of presents this year!"

The friends watched as Jack Frost rolled up the scroll and stuck it back in his pocket.

"If I can't write on this old scrap, I'll find someone who can," said Jack Frost, his ice-cold eyes glinting with determination. "This place is crawling with doctors and nurses. All we've got to do is trick one of them into writing my name for me. Someone sickeningly good like them should get the magic going!"

The goblins started to laugh.

"*Sick*-eningly good!" snorted one. "Nice hospital joke!"

The other clutched his belly and began to hoot with laughter.

Jack Frost didn't even crack a smile. Instead he grabbed both goblins by their shirts and yanked them down behind the bed.

"Someone's coming!" he hissed, ducking out of sight.

There was the sound of footsteps and the creak of a door being pushed open.

"Oh no," gasped Kirsty. "It's the doctor we saw earlier!"

The girls shared an alarmed look. Now they'd never get the scroll back!

Three New Patients

"Is anyone in here?" called the doctor, flicking on the main light. "This ward should be closed."

Jack Frost leapt out from behind the bed, hastily straightening his worker's uniform coat.

"Just us hospital workers," he lied. "We're giving the place a good clean. Got to keep it nice for the children, right?"

The two goblins looked at each other

shiftily. Jack Frost shot them such a fierce glare that they started clumsily making one of the beds. Angelica and her friends flitted up out of sight.

Jack Frost turned back to the doctor. "I'm sure you got the memo," he insisted, pulling the enchanted scroll out of his pocket. "All you have to do is sign here and we'll have this place looking tip-top for your next group of patients."

The doctor looked uneasy.

"Hurry up," pressed one of the goblins. "We've got work to do."

Angelica covered her worried eyes.

"This isn't how the enchanted scroll should be treated," she cried. "I can't bear to look!" Jack Frost handed the pen to the doctor. Kirsty and Rachel clutched Angelica's hands.

"I'll sign that form later," the doctor announced, taking the pen. "You three need a prescription first!"

Jack Frost's lip began to tremble.

"Wh-what's a *prescription*?" he stammered.

The doctor pulled a pad out of his pocket. "It's a list of medicines I want you to take. I've never seen anyone so off-color!"

Before they could argue, Jack Frost and

the goblins found themselves being helped into hospital beds. The doctor put a thermometer into Jack Frost's mouth, then walked around to examine the goblins.

"Say *ahhh*!" he muttered. "You're practically *green*. You must be feeling really sick."

"Now that you mention it, I do," said the goblin with the long nose.

"Am I going to be OK, Doc?" asked the other goblin.

Kirsty did a somersault in the air. "Jack Frost's plan is backfiring!" she said.

"Now those
silly goblins
really think
that they're
sick," added
Angelica, trying
not to giggle.

Kirsty blinked with surprise as the
doctor pulled the thermometer out of
Jack Frost's mouth. There was a tinkly,
splitting sound — the glass tube had
frozen solid!

"That's impossible!" said the stunned
doctor, rubbing his eyes and checking
again. "How can it give me a minus
reading? Let's get you wrapped up nice
and warm."

Rachel stifled a laugh as the doctor
piled blankets and hot water bottles into

Jack Frost's bed. His spiky hair and beard began to droop and his nose turned a funny shade of pink.

"I think I'm melting!" he wailed. "Stop it!"

Luckily, this doctor was used to difficult patients. He tucked all three in extra

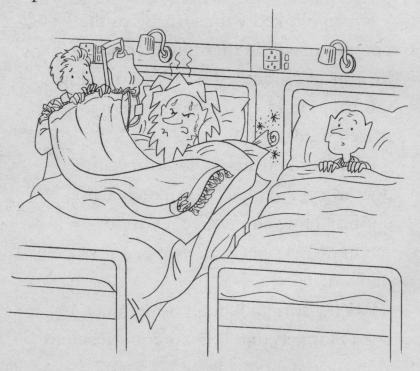

tight, telling them that they should be fine as long as they rested up for a week or two. By the time he headed back off on his rounds, the trio really thought they were sick!

"That's it, then." The long nosed goblin groaned. "Christmas is canceled!"

Angelica pointed down to Jack Frost's bed — she could still see the enchanted scroll sticking out from under the covers.

"Should we fly down and get it?" she suggested.

Kirsty's eyes began to twinkle. "I have an even better idea," she replied.

The Nice List

Kirsty took Rachel's and Angelica's hands.

"If we can persuade Jack Frost to give the enchanted scroll back, his name might appear on the parchment all by itself," she whispered.

Angelica nodded. "That way Santa will remember to bring him some presents, too."

"Let's give Jack Frost a chance to do something good," agreed Rachel.

The friends darted out from their hiding spot.

The goblins began to howl as soon as they saw the trails of golden fairy dust shimmering above their beds.

"Call the doctor back!" yelled the one with the long nose. "I'm starting to see things!"

"Not *things*," said Kirsty, "*fairies*!"

Angelica hovered over Jack Frost's bed. "Please, may I have my enchanted scroll

back?" she asked sweetly. "There's still enough time to make sure that the children here and all over the world get the Christmas presents they deserve."

Jack Frost stuck out his tongue. "No! What about the presents *I* deserve?"

Rachel plucked up all her courage, then fluttered a little closer.

"This is your chance to get off the naughty list," she urged. "If you give the scroll back to Angelica, your name might appear on Santa's list."

Jack Frost hesitated for a moment.

"It only takes one good deed to make the magic work," Angelica said.

"Time is running out," called Kirsty. "It's now or never!"

Angelica held out both hands and waited patiently.

Jack Frost scowled, then pulled the scroll out from under the covers.

"All right." He grimaced. "Take the silly thing!"

The instant the scroll left his hands, the parchment shrank back down to fairy-size.

"Thank you!" cried Angelica, clutching the magic object to her chest.

Kirsty and Rachel watched spellbound as Angelica carefully undid the red velvet ribbon and unraveled the enchanted scroll. Even Jack Frost peeked nervously over his blankets.

Angelica ran her tiny fingertip down the list of names. There were thousands, each written in beautiful fountain pen. Her finger stopped halfway down the page.

"Here you are," she read carefully. "Frost, Jack."

Jack Frost couldn't help but grin. He even pushed himself up in the bed and high-fived the goblins!

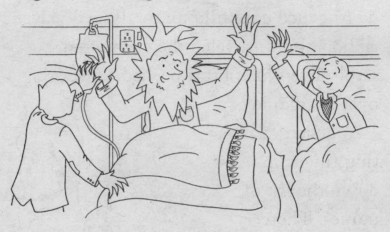

"It's time to go back to your Ice Castle," said Angelica, "but when you wake up tomorrow morning there might be a few surprises waiting for you!"

A fountain of glittering swirls cascaded out of Angelica's wand, bathing Jack Frost and his goblins in an exquisite golden light.

Jack Frost muttered something quietly.

"What was that?" asked Kirsty.

Jack Frost lifted his arms into the air, then summoned the two goblins to stand close.

"If you must know," he snapped, "I said, *Happy holidays!*"

There was a crack of lightning and the trio was gone.

"I never thought I'd hear Jack Frost talk like that," marveled Angelica, rolling the scroll up and tucking it under her arm. "What a perfect end to our adventure together!"

"The adventure's not over quite yet," Kirsty reminded her. "You need to take the enchanted scroll to the North Pole. Santa will be waiting!"

At that moment, the sound of children's laughter started to echo down the corridor.

"And we need to help the Brownies give out those presents!" Rachel beamed.

"Let's hurry," added Kirsty. "The children need to get to bed on time. It *is* Christmas Eve!"

With a tap of her wand, Angelica changed Kirsty and Rachel back to their normal size.

"Good-bye," cried Rachel. "Happy holidays!"

Angelica waved her magic wand one last time. A beautiful soft doll with fairy wings suddenly appeared in Kirsty's outstretched hand. The doll had auburn hair and a frothy white dress, just like Angelica's!

"A special present." She winked. "For a little girl named Emily."

SPECIAL EDITION

Don't miss any of Rachel and Kirsty's
other fairy adventures!
Check out this magical sneak peek of

Rachel Walker strolled over to the grand
doors of Tippington Town Hall and
peered outside. There were buses pulling
up and lots of people milling around, but
no sign of the very special person she was
looking for, her best friend, Kirsty Tate!

Rachel's school was taking part in
an exciting competition. Four schools
from different parts of the country were
competing in two different events; a
spelling bee was going to be held today at
Tippington Town Hall and a science fair
was to take place at the Science Museum
tomorrow. At the end of the week, there
would be a dance at Rachel's school!

Rachel was part of the Tippington
School spelling bee team, but the *most*
exciting thing was that Kirsty's school was
also taking part in the competition. Kirsty
was part of the science team and this
meant that she was coming to Tippington!

"Rachel! Over here!" called Kirsty.
Rachel turned around and there was
Kirsty! She was standing with three

other children and a friendly-looking teacher.

"There you are! I was wondering when you'd get here!" said Rachel, running over to Kirsty and giving her a big hug.

"We came in through the side entrance," said Kirsty with a smile. "This is my teacher, Mrs. Richards, and this is my science team!"

Just then, an official-looking man in a fancy suit appeared on the stairs leading up to the auditorium. "Attention please, everyone! I am your host for today's competition. Will the four teams taking part in the competition please make their way to the backstage area? Members of the audience should take their seats in the auditorium."

The four spelling bee teams started to make their way to the backstage area.

"I'll join you in a minute!" Rachel called to her team. "I'm just going to walk Kirsty to her seat."

The girls split off from the main group of students and teachers in the hall, and made their way toward a side entrance. As they strolled along, something in one of the trophy cases caught Kirsty's eye. "Rachel, what *is* that?" she asked, stepping closer.

"It's just the light shining on the Tippington in Bloom cup, isn't it?" replied Rachel, still walking toward the auditorium.

"I think it's something even more special than that!" whispered Kirsty happily, tugging on Rachel's arm. Rachel stopped suddenly. There, sitting on the edge of a shiny trophy surrounded by a magical glow, was a beautiful little fairy!

RAINBOW magic™

Which Magical Fairies Have You Met?

- ❑ The Rainbow Fairies
- ❑ The Weather Fairies
- ❑ The Jewel Fairies
- ❑ The Pet Fairies
- ❑ The Dance Fairies
- ❑ The Music Fairies
- ❑ The Sports Fairies
- ❑ The Party Fairies
- ❑ The Ocean Fairies
- ❑ The Night Fairies
- ❑ The Magical Animal Fairies
- ❑ The Princess Fairies
- ❑ The Superstar Fairies
- ❑ The Fashion Fairies
- ❑ The Sugar & Spice Fairies
- ❑ The Earth Fairies
- ❑ The Magical Crafts Fairies
- ❑ The Baby Animal Rescue Fairies

■ SCHOLASTIC

Find all of your favorite fairy friends at
scholastic.com/rainbowmagic

HIT entertainment

RMFAIRY12